BOOK 1: VIRTUA

VIRTUALLY
SLEEPING BEAUTY

K.M. ROBINSON

To those with big wishes,
Don't wait around for others—build your own empire, you
dreamer, you!
You've got this!

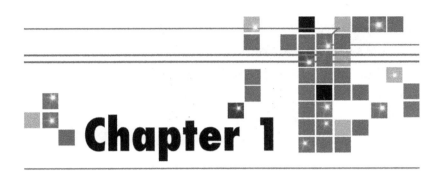

Chapter 1

"I can't get her up," she sounds panicked.

"You can't *what?*" I mumble.

"I can't get her up, Royce. You need to come over here and help me."

She sounds like she's rushing around the room. Suddenly, I hear the sound of skin coming in contact with skin as she taps her goddaughter's cheek repeatedly as she tries to wake her.

"Would you relax please, Aunt Perry? She's in a game. She'll be under for a while. That's just how virtual reality works these days—once you're in the chair, you're out for up to four hours depending on your settings."

I jingle my keys to my car, trying to flip to the correct one. It's ridiculous how many different keys I have to carry for my family.

"That's the problem, Royce. She's been in there since this morning."

I glance at my watch. 3 pm.

"What *time* this morning?" A twinge of nervousness slips

into my voice. I don't exactly know this girl, but that fact that she's been in for over four hours has me concerned.

"Eight. She was supposed to be out for lunch. We had errands to run."

Perry murmurs something to the girl, this time slapping her harder.

"Perry, stop!" I shout. "That's not going to help."

"What about water—?"

"No!" I bellow. "Just stop messing with her. I'll be right over."

I drop my coffee cup into the drink holder before slamming the keys into the ignition. The car roars to life—*the red-hot beauty that she is*—and I take off down the block.

Aunt Perry's house is only a few streets away but by the time I arrive, she's in the driveway waving hysterically at me. I take a deep breath to steel myself.

"Royce, I don't know what's happening," she sobs as she grabs my arm, pulling me toward the house. My coffee sloshes out of the mouthpiece of my container, dripping on my hand. Good thing it wasn't that hot to begin with.

We stumble up the steps clumsily as she pulls me into the house. My father's siblings have never been known for being great in a crisis. She pulls me toward the stairs inside and I managed to pull free of her so I can walk with my drippy hand on the banister.

"Calm down, we'll handle it," I demand a little more aggressively than I mean to. Perry looks close to tears. "I'm sorry. We'll figure this out, I just need you to stop shouting."

She nods, holding back the tears.

"Okay, tell me what happened," I prompt.

"Rora has been staying with me this week while her parents are on their trip," Perry starts, gaining the tiniest semblance of the ability to speak. "Once or twice in the evenings she's played her game for an hour, but she always comes down to have ice cream with me before we go to bed."

None of this is helpful, but okay.

"Because it's the weekend, she usually gets up early to play, so we had planned on her playing until eleven and then we were going to go get lunch and run some errands. When I came to check on her a little after eleven, she was still in the game. I assumed she started late so I gave her an extra hour."

She tugs me over to the sleeping girl in the chair, sniffling.

"It's been hours, Royce. I can't wake her up. What do we do?"

"Some people have been known to take extra injections to stay in longer," I offer.

"She wouldn't. She's too responsible for that." Perry gives me an impatient look. "This is the girl who is class president, and works at charities, and does all of her homework for the entire week before she even *considers* playing a virtual game. Rora wouldn't take extra injections when she knows it's against the rules."

Some people are adrenaline junkies—they do it for the

rush. Maybe Rora is one of those girls who is super straight-laced in all other parts of her life and this is her guilty pleasure.

I can't say that would be the *worst* thing in the world. I, myself, would love to stay in the games longer.

"Well, if that's the case, maybe we should call a medical team to come wake her up," I reply, turning for the door. Let them handle her.

"No!" Perry shouts, racing after me. "We can't. If some-thing really *did* happen, we can't let them catch her. And even if she hasn't done anything wrong, her mother's going to kill me for letting this happen on my watch. Please, Royce, we need a better idea."

I sigh dramatically.

I don't like being at everyone's beck and call.

"Fine, there's one other thing we can do first."

Setting my coffee cup on the desk next to a few of the girl's binders, I walk back over to where she's quietly laying in the chair.

She's still breathing, which is a good sign. Her fingers twitch slightly so I can tell she's playing the game. Other than that, she barely moves—a side effect of the injections that allow us to enter the virtual world and feel and experi-ence everything inside the game.

"I'll go in and find her," I announce.

"What? No, Royce, you can't." My aunt pulls on my arm. "What if you get stuck in there too?"

"I won't. I do this all the time." I brush her off. "Go grab me an injection, would you?"

After an angry look, she turns and leaves to find an injection.

Most people use the virtual reality system in one form or another, so there are usually injections lying around every house. The older generation uses it to relax—sometimes they go to a beach, other times they attend orchestra concerts or explore museums. The younger generations are more careless and play high intensity games. I tend to spend my time gaining skills I'll never use in real life as I leap from buildings and save damsels in distress.

I climb into the chair next to her and roll up my sleeve. When I have my feet comfortably arranged at the end of the footrest, I lean back and make sure I like the position I'm sitting in.

Perry walks back in and hands me the injection.

"I'm going to set the machine for an hour, but hopefully I'll find her right away. I need to get over to Alan's, so I don't have a lot of time to waste."

Perry looks nervous so I send her downstairs with the assignment of running her errands for the day. I promise to call her when I have her houseguest back in the real world. She reluctantly agrees to leave, slowly walking out the door to her car. An empty house is for the best right now.

I wait for her to drive away. The last thing I need is for her to come back in, have a meltdown, and throw water on me while I'm in the game. I quietly study the girl's face while I wait so that I don't accidentally miss her in the game. It's a little hard to see around her goggles, but it will suffice. I program the machine to take me to the game she is playing.

With the headset on, ready to be slipped over my eyes, I place my hand on the reader to identify myself and then inject my arm. I quickly put the goggles in place and rest my hands on the arms of the chair.

My vision goes black before crackling into a white burst of light. It fizzles out as the gamescape filters into place in front of me.

Interestingly enough, Rora plays the same game that I do. That should make this easier.

I glance down at my armor to make sure everything is in place. My weapons are just as I left them, attached to the quiver on my back. When I'm sure nothing glitched on me, I walk forward into the game, leaving the holding cell behind. It disappears behind me, evaporating into the air, leaving me exposed.

I quickly flip my settings to explore mode, preventing me from losing any of my credits in the game. I can't engage with people and earn items within the game, but I can walk around and talk to them. It's not something the game allows you to do for extended periods of time, but occasionally people use the setting to meet with their friends while they were in different locations, so the game gives us some leniency while we wait for people to show up.

Now, I just have to figure out where to find the girl.

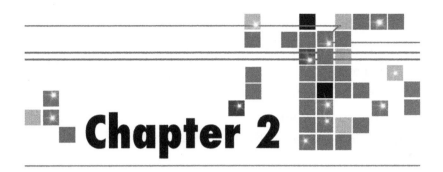

Chapter 2

THE LAST TIME I WALKED AROUND WITHOUT PLAYING WAS when I had to wait for Alan to bother to show up for a team round. It was so long ago, that I've forgotten how funny it is to watch newer players try to rank in the game—so many easy mistakes.

I wish I had been able to bring my coffee with me—it could have been a nice, leisurely stroll through the kingdom. I shouldn't waste time meandering around though. Find the girl; get out.

I wonder if she'll let me ping her location.

Pulling up my controls, I enter her screen name that I cleverly looked at before entering the game. When Rora-Rose registers, I request her coordinates. Hopefully she'll recognize me as Perry's nephew.

While I wait for a reply, I walk toward the castle. The next time I'm in the game, my mission is going to take me there. I have to figure out how to get in, so a little reconnaissance mission while I wait to hear from Rora won't hurt.

Everything inside the gamescape is brighter that in the real world. Buildings are taller. Lines are sharper.

It's magnificent.

To my left a girl is screaming, running from a battle with an ogre. She has an axe and could easily take it out, but apparently today is not her day.

Off to the right is one of my classmates, Harry. He and Gina appear to be on a quest. It looks like Gina is taking it easy so Harry can keep up—*the downfalls of playing with your boyfriend*. I try not to embarrass him when Gina stares. She and I have played together once before and I don't want to take any of the spotlight off of Harry because she knows I'm easier to work with.

Several young teens run past me, dressed in breastplates and leather pants. They'll learn the benefits of a suit of armor soon enough. While it doesn't look as modern as their attire, it's better for battle.

An electrical pulse snaps across the control panel on my wrist—I'm receiving a message.

Coordinates appear on the screen, telling me where Rora is located. Surprisingly, I'm going the right way.

I continue on my path, this time much faster than before. Several young girls stare as I walk by, glancing at the sword on my hip. I wave as I pass.

"Really, Royce, you couldn't pick anything that glares less in the sun?" Alan asks, sidling up to me.

"Where did you come from?" I ask, realizing I now have help on my mission.

"I got your text message and thought you might need a hand with the little lady." We fall into step.

"You realize we're both wearing the same thing, right?"

"Yours is gold. It glares in the sun. Mine is black and doesn't shine at all," Alan informs me, knocking his hand against his metal-covered chest.

"Makes sense. Only one of us can shine at a time." I grin at him sarcastically.

Alan makes a face but defers tackling me until our mission is over. We pick up the pace as we track Rora's coordinates.

"So who is this girl we're searching for?"

"Perry's goddaughter. Her name is Rora. Apparently she went into the game this morning and still hasn't come back out."

"How did she manage that? Did she over-juice?"

"Doesn't look like it. We'll find out when we ask her though. She should be just around the corner in the trading post."

A knave stands on the corner, looking for a fight. When he sees us, he runs, sword out in front of him. He swings it at us as he yells, but it bounces off the invisible shield that surrounds us while we're in explore mode. The metal vibrates in his hands as it bounces back.

"Sorry, we're just here to talk to someone," I inform him as he snarls at us.

"You won't be so lucky next time," he scowls before scampering away.

"Why do the knaves always think they can take on a knight?" Alan shakes his head. "Let alone two of us. Like we didn't see him coming."

I roll my eyes. They'll never learn.

The trading post is filled with people. It's hard to hear over the voices chattering around us.

"Wait here," I instruct Alan.

Inside is even more crowded. I muscle my way through, looking for the blonde princess.

"Hey there, handsome," a woman says. She's at least five years older than me.

"Hello, ma'am," I nod, trying to brush past her.

"Where ya going, Mr. Knight?"

"I'm looking for someone, sorry."

The raven-haired gypsy follows me around the post. Every time I look back, she's on my tail.

"I'm really busy, sorry," I try brushing her off again.

"You *will* be," she murmurs, wandering away.

Spices fill the air, mixed with the scent of leather and blood. When you're injured in the game, you suffer the pain until you return to the real world. The place is crowded with new players looking for bandages and potions.

"I'm looking for RoraRose. Have you seen her?" I ask the man working the exchange register.

"She was here a while ago. I don't know where she went." He shrugs, waiting to take credits from the next person in line.

"Hey, Royce!" Alan calls from outside.

I push my way through the crowd, feeling an instant drop in temperature the moment I step outside of the crowded building.

Pressed against one of the support columns that holds up the front of the porch, a blonde dressed in purple and black pants with a half skirt wrapped around it stares at me. Her arms are crossed, one foot kicked up against the column with her knee bent. The girl's collar arches up over her shoulder and wraps magnificently around the hair piled on top of her head. A few loose curls hang down in a way that is unmistakably soft and girly *and* harsh and foreboding all at one.

Her gaze looks like it could cut down any man in its path.

"Really? *You're* Royce? Some prince you turned out to be," she scoffs. "It's about time somebody showed up."

"Rora," I regard her, nodding once. "Perry is beside herself. Do you have any idea what you've put her through?"

I cross my arms, mimicking her. She is nothing like I expected her to be.

"I'm locked in. I don't know what happened," she drops her tough girl act. "I should have been pulled out hours ago and it won't let me return manually."

"Anything we should know?" Alan charmingly asks. *Idiot.*

She glares at him in disgust.

"Never mind, I'll figure it out on my own." She turns to stomp away.

"Hold up," I reach for her, catching her elbow. "He didn't

mean to accuse you of anything. We can't leave without you, so let's figure this out."

"He most certainly did," she snarls at him. She's feisty. "For the record, I didn't do anything to cause this. I didn't juice and I never would. I'm not sure why I'm in here."

"Did you make a bad trade with someone? Could it have been some kind of glitch in the system?"

"Have you ever known the system to glitch before?" Rora's eyes spark as she speaks. "As far as I know, no one has ever been locked inside the system. My last trade was with a magician. Everything seemed to work properly. It wasn't even today...it was two days ago."

She blinks impertinently at me as she waits for a response. When the light bounces off my armor and reflects onto her face, it lights up the little flecks that sparkle in her dramatic eye makeup.

"Let's talk to the magician," I suggest. Maybe he knows something."

"*She* may not even be in the game right now."

I hold my hands up to apologize for assuming, though mainly it's to keep from being pummeled. She looks like she'd have no trouble feeding me to the dragons.

Just then, a large flame rises in the air in the distance. *Speaking of dragons...*

I extend my hand, gesturing that we should start walking. Rora and Alan turn and the three of us start toward the castle where the magicians can usually be found hiding in the dark corners just outside the moat.

Rora's half skirt trails behind her as she walks, making her look like she would fit right in with the royalty inside the castle. Alan elbows me as we walk behind her. The dagger that dangles on her hip might have warned him off if we weren't in explore mode.

"I've tried using all of the escape buttons," Rora calls over her shoulder, prompting us to walk faster and catch up to her. "I've even tried pausing the game, but it hasn't done anything."

A scream rises up to our right as a girl with a spear charges at Rora. Alan and I watch as she sprints I our direction, weapon in the air. We're shocked when Rora engages with her.

She pulls her dagger from her hip, knowing her arrows won't be fast enough to stop the oncoming attack. Rora ducks, using her arm to block the spear before it can touch her. She hits the ground and rolls, bouncing to her feet before the girl can take her on.

Rora kicks the girl's leg, shattering it as the girl crumples on the ground. In a moment of pure rage, the girl thrusts her spear at Rora, nicking her arm. Blood bubbles up from the ripped sleeve of her dark outfit.

"What are you doing?" I shout, rushing to her side.

"I can't enter explore mode," Rora shrieks desperately, trying to cradle her arm and take on her attacker at the same time.

Two more people run out from an alley, ready to target Rora. I quickly take myself out of explore mode and prepare to defend her. Alan joins me, making it an unfair match for the geniuses that thought they could take us on.

The moment she sees us enter the game, Rora straightens, throwing down her arm to her side in a show of strength. She reaches behind her for her bow, but one of the boys reaches her first. Rora kicks at him, knocking him back. As he comes at her again, she lands a punch to his nose, breaking it with a loud crunch. He's going to be incredibly thankful injuries don't follow us into the real world.

I wield my sword, clashing with the first assassin who ran from the shadows. He's quick, but not as quick as I am. His weapon falls to the ground and I slam my sword into it, making it vanish from the game.

He takes a step back as I lunge toward him. Thinking better of it, he turns and runs, taking his partner with him. I'm not done with them yet though.

"Get them," I instruct Alan before turning back to Rora to see how bad the damage is. Alan rushes after the assassins. "Are you okay?"

"I'm fine," she says, cradling her arm.

"Do you have health points?" I inquire.

"Yeah, but at the rate I'm going, I think I should save them for when something worse happens."

She purses her lips. She's not telling me something.

"You've already been attacked today…"

She nods, finally making eye contact with me.

"Earlier. Before you got here. One of those guys came

after me. I tried hiding in the crowd at the trading post, but that didn't go so well. Apparently he found me. I only gave you my location because I connected you with Perry."

"Let me see your arm." I hold out my hand to her. It takes a moment, but she finally relinquishes it.

"Really, it's fine," she protests. She doesn't like relying on other people.

"Let's see if you can look for an Apple of Life. That would fix this right up and you wouldn't have to waste your health points."

She nods and allows me to guide her to a small cluster of trees near the water pump in the center of town. I almost leave her on a stone bench by the pump, but think better of it in case Alan hasn't caught the assassins yet—we need information before we leave her alone again.

"There," she says, pointing high above our heads. "Give me a boost."

I lower my hands, weaving my fingers together. She runs at me, placing her foot in my hand. I lift her and she flies toward the tree. Her foot hits it and she bounces off, high into the branches. She's playing as a princess, but she has the skill sets of a ninja.

Grasping the Apple of Life, she allows gravity to do its work, falling out of the tree. Her feet hit the ground and she crouches into what looks like the beginnings of a pounce. Like a cat, she gracefully springs back up and slinks over to me, twisting the apple in her hand.

Rora clenches it hard in her hand—claiming her points —making it disappear. The mark on her arm instantly heals.

"Easy enough. Thanks for the hand." She brushes her sleeve off as if something still remained where she had been injured. "Good as new."

"Tell them," Alan rushes up, an assassin's cape in his clutch.

"She has a bounty on her head," the younger of the assassins informs us. "The entire game will be coming after her soon. They just set the challenge to the assassins first."

"What's the price?" Rora asks, crossing her arms as she strides up to him.

"Everything you have," he sneers at her, looking like he wants to shatter her.

I backhand him.

He falls to the ground, temporarily knocked out of the game until he regenerates with one less life point.

"What are you doing?" Rora shrieks, grabbing my arm as if I would hit him again. "He could have told us why."

"That's all he knew," Alan says, shaking his head.

"So what now?" she mumbles. "Why are they after me?"

"What will the acquire if they kill you?"

She pauses as if she doesn't want to say.

"We can't help unless we know what's going on," I remind her.

"Everything. They're getting everything. I'm one of the highest ranked players in this game."

"Yeah, okay," Alan scoffs. "If you're so important, why haven't we heard of you?"

"An intelligent woman knows when to keep her secrets. I've been quietly playing this game for as long as you two have—I just don't go around bragging about it. I don't take on challenges for the sake of taking on challenges. I'm strategic. I've been saving up for the final battle—I'm close. I could rule the castle soon, if I wanted."

"You're going to take on the Queen?" I try not to sound sarcastic. I fail.

She stares at me as she taps a button on her control panel. A translucent screen pops up with a list of all her battles, challenges, statistics, and the items she has collected along the way.

Rora is as skilled as I am.

For once, Alan has nothing to say.

That is, until an angry mob of half a dozen people come running around the corner from behind a large pink building, screaming for Rora's head. We prepare to fight them, but before we can, Alan starts glitching.

"Not now!" he yells, tapping on his control panel. He tries to warn us as he fades away. "I'm being pulled out!"

He must have set his timer for less time than I did.

"This is bad," I say, pulling my sword.

Rora rips her bow off her back and takes aim.

"I hate this part," she informs me before releasing an arrow at the mob.

My sword clashes against a shield as a guy my age tries

to get around me to reach Rora. When I look over, she's surrounded. Someone tries to grab her around the waist.

"Behind you!" I shout as I kick at the person in front of me. She struggles to evade him.

Then, suddenly, it's like she's changed modes. She effortlessly fights the other players off, taking them out left and right. Rora elbows a knave, knocking him down before using her dagger to fend off a girl a decade older than us.

We're down to five people left when I feel the tug. My hand starts to disappear, my skin glitching in and out of the game.

"No!"

My shout makes Rora whip around to face me.

"I'll be back! I'll find you!" I shout as I'm torn from the game, leaving her alone to take on the remaining assassins.

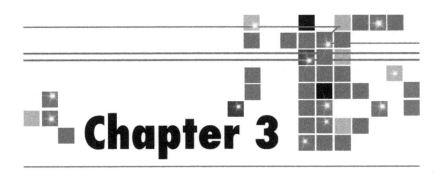

Chapter 3

I WAKE UP WITH A START. RIPPING THE GOGGLES OFF, I PUNCH my fingers against the control panel to pull up my logs. I hope Rora stays in the same general area so I can find her.

The game has a lock that won't allow us to go back into the game for an hour—it's an hour that might kill me.

My phone buzzes next to me—Alan.

"You're out?" he demands as soon as I answer.

"It pulled me," I confirm. "She's all alone taking on those assassins. We have to get back in there."

"From what I saw in her logs, she can handle herself, but I'm on my way over. For now, see if you can find a way to wake her up from this side." The phone clicks off.

She's still in the chair next to me, fingers twitching once in a while as she plays.

"Rora?" I hover over her. "Rora, can you hear me? I'm coming back for you, just stay safe until then."

I try picking her hand up to see if the movement would wake her, but her muscles are stiff, as if they're part of the chair arm. I wonder if my muscles lock like that too while I'm in the game.

My eyes dart around the room looking for an idea. Somehow I don't think a bunch of bookshelves will help me. *Waiting* may be the only thing I *can* do.

The door opens downstairs. I assume it will be Alan walking in, but once I reach the landing, I discover that it's Aunt Perry.

"Is she out?" Perry demands, setting down two large bags on the small table by the door. I fear the table might collapse under the weight of the groceries.

"I went in and talked to her. She's locked inside the game. Alan and I got pulled out, but we're going back in for her as soon as the timer lets us."

Perry twists her fingers nervously. When she starts pacing around the room, I launch myself down the steps. I scoop up the bags and thrust one of them at her. I hold on to the other.

"You need to put this away. Whatever is going on here, it's not right. Rora didn't do anything that would cause her to get stuck, but we can't let anyone know about this." I push at Perry's back to make her move toward the kitchen. "Put these away and then go next door to visit Mr. Grimmerson. Stay there for a few hours while Alan and I work on getting her out of the game."

Perry nods but it doesn't look like she's heard a word I've said.

"Aunt Perry, did you hear me?"

"Her parents are going to kill me," she says through tears.

"No, they won't because she'll be just fine. She's one of the best players in that game. They can't touch her."

"What do you mean? Is she getting hurt in there?" Perry suddenly grows coherent.

"She'll be fine. We just need to wake her up, that's all. We're going to help her get out. Just go next door, please."

"I'm here," Alan slams through the door. He takes one look at Perry and looks like he's going to bolt.

"Upstairs," I point quickly before ushering my aunt to the door. "Just go to see Mr. Grimmerson and don't come back until you see Alan or I out in the yard, okay? Grimmerson is a talker so you should be fine."

"But..." she objects.

"Just go, Aunt Perry. I promise I'll wake her up."

I carefully force her out the door and shut it behind her. When she turns back to me, I wave her along. She reluctantly goes to her neighbor's.

I turn, throwing anything cold into the refrigerator before rushing up the stairs.

"It kind of has a creepy look to it now, doesn't it?" Alan asks without turning around to face me. "If she wasn't twitching, I'd think she were dead."

"She's not dead," I murmur as I grab to injections and place them on the armrests of the chairs. "We just need to get back in there."

"Should we both go at the same time? We only have

three hours left each." Alan's point strikes like lightning, making me swallow.

"That's a good point. If we can't get her out, at least we can protect her longer." My breathing is shallower than it should be as my mind tumbles over ideas for saving her. I need to remember to breath.

"We can't let her stay in there all day though. There's no telling what it's doing to her body out here while she's under the influence of the game. It could have lasting effects." Alan has always been the more practical of us.

I glance at Rora as she sits in the chair. Her shell is here, but *she* is elsewhere, possibly in danger. Every minute that she doesn't return makes me more nervous.

"I'll go in first," I reply. "You stay here and research. See if this has ever happened before and if it has, what they did to fix it. And *don't* get caught. No one is going to believe someone who has achieved that much in the game didn't turn to juicing to stay in longer."

"I'll be careful," he nods, looking at Rora. "Just make sure you're careful in there too. You actually have to play the game and there's an angry group of people out to kill."

"I can afford a few lives," I remind him.

"Yeah, but you only get three a day, so don't blow it."

He makes a good point.

I glance at my cup of coffee on the desk. So much for it still being warm. I turn back to face Rora as Alan pulls up a search on his phone to start working. I set a timer on my phone—ten more minutes.

After the longest ten minutes of my life, the timer finally goes off. I jump into the chair next to Rora and put the headpiece on.

"Hey, just remember, you don't have to save her. She's fine on her own, so you're just there to help her. There's no reason to be a big, tough hero in there," Alan reminds me. He grins sneakily before adding, "That's *my* job."

"Whatever, man," I say as I inject myself. "See you in three hours. Watch over her. If something goes wrong, it doesn't matter—just get help. We'll deal with the consequences later..."

My words trail off as I fade into the game.

I arrive back where I left Rora but she's nowhere to be found. The thugs have moved on. The game cleaned up whatever wreckage there was so I can't even tell if she's been hurt.

Taping on my control panel, I try to contact her. It comes up as static.

"This is bad," I mumble to myself.

I need information. By now, everyone has to have the kill challenge. I only make it three steps before it pops up in my control panel.

Ducking into the shadows of the pink building, I read the instructions. Two hundred players have already checked in to the challenge list. She'll have to survive them all, but at least the challenge is still being handed out which means she hasn't been caught yet.

Whoever wants her gone is really gunning for her.

I try to contact her again, but it's still nothing but static. I type a message telling her I'm going to the castle to look for the magician in case it manages to get through to her.

I bat at a vine hanging down from the top of the building. The greenery against the pink of the tower makes it look like a giant watermelon. Then again, the tall vines nearly look like bamboo, so who knows what I'm really looking at. The branch swings back quietly, like a lock of a girl's hair in the breeze.

I peel out of the alleyway and move quickly toward the castle. Unfortunately, I already used my one explore mode use for the day, so I'm hyper-vigilant to take in my surroundings. Most people will be focused on catching Rora, but I'm high ranking as well and an easy pick if I'm distracted.

Ahead, the random tree in the middle of the town shifts shapes. An Apple of Life grows on a low branch. I have a feeling that I might need it, so I jog over. When an assassin appears, also running toward it, I attack. I don't need the Apple of life so much that I'm willing to take out an assassin for it, but I know he will be going after Rora when he's done and it's easier to take him out now.

I'm worried about what will happen to Rora's physical body if she's trapped in the game much longer. Alan's point is a scary reminder that we don't know what all of this means. Even worse, I'm terrified over what might happen if Rora depletes all of her lives inside the game and is still trapped.

The assassin launches himself at me, trying to punch my face. I duck, pulling a branch back. When I release it, it snaps in his eyes. He reels back, blinded by the branches.

By the time I'm done, he's been pulled from the game for the day. I pluck the Apple of Life off the tree and take off down the now-quiet street.

Most people leave me alone as I run down the dirt roads. On normal days, if someone is running and it's not at you, it's best not to get involved. Today, most people have a goal in mind and if I'm not going to help them catch Rora, they don't pay any attention.

When I reach the edge of town, I spot a warlock trying to create a team of fighters to go after Rora. He shouts loudly to organize them. Wasting time trying to disband them would be a mistake, so I keep running through the rows of tall pink buildings covered in vines.

It's beyond me who decided pink was a good color for a building, but the kingdom is paved with them. Each one is a twisted shape with long, dark shadows. Some crumble with virtually assigned age, showing the wear of battles long since fought. Ahead, the castle glimmers in the sunlight, a pale blue color that I assume is supposed to be symbolic of glass.

The water in the moat sparkles a dark navy blue with crests of white as if it were the ocean. Despite the lack of a breeze, it ripples fiercely.

I pause for a moment, scouting the bridge that leads across the outer moat. Players are allowed to cross the outer moat and enter the kingdom courtyard, but only players on quests that involve the castle can go beyond that and cross the second bridge to the castle grounds. I've been theee twice before.

People are bustling on the wide bridge, trading and forming alliances. I let my hand linger near my sword as I step onto the dark brown wood of the bridge.

I weave my way through the crowd, trying to find any sign that Rora has come this way. She's not on the bridge, but when I reach the grass, I make my way to the shadows where I might find the magician.

"Hello," I greet someone in a deep red cloak. They turn and I find another princess, this one in full ball gown.

"Hello," she says cautiously.

"I'm sorry, I thought you were someone else," I excuse myself. She quickly wanders away.

She had the same hair color, so it was logical to think it might have been her. Rationalizing is a strong suit of mine.

Deeper into a recess behind one of the sculptures large enough to be a room, I find someone covered in darkness. Something pricks along my arm, urging me forward.

"I'm looking for a magician," I call.

The figure shuffles further back, trying to get away from me.

"Please, I require a magicians help," I say again, this time softer to show I am not a threat.

The figure pauses, waiting for me to approach. The hood on their cloak conceals their face, but I think I've found my magic woman. I place my hand on the hilt of my sword just in case.

Fingers wrap around my shoulders, slamming me backward into a corner. I can't unsheathe my sword, so my dagger will have to do.

"Shhh," she hisses. "Put that away."

"Rora," I gasp.

"Of course, you fool. Who did you think I was?" She scowls in the shadows.

She must not have recognized me when I first walked in.

"Where did you get a cloak from?" I question, looking her over. "And how did you fit it over that massive collar?"

"It doesn't matter, I did." Her fingers are still on me. It's impossible to feel her touch through my armor, but I feel every single finger as it rests on me. "It certainly took you long enough."

"I've been trying to find you for twenty minutes," I say, annoyed.

"I found the magician," she says, not noticing my dig. "She's over there."

"Great, let's go talk to her."

"Wait," she tugs on me as I try to turn away. "I can't go out there."

I pause, examining her.

"You're worried about what happens to you out there," I muse. She nods. "I have Alan researching that now, but honestly, we're kind of worried too—you're barely breathing out there." I ignore the part where she looks like she could be dead—there's no need to worry her over that.

"He'll send a message in if he finds anything," I add.

The game allows people who are friends within the game to send short messages to each other inside the game in order to coordinate missions. For some people, it's their only form of communication because they don't have contact in the outside world.

Rora glances around me, looking at the magician.

"I'll go talk to her, you stay here."

I leave her in the dark corner, hoping she watches me walk away. I make sure to give her a good show.

The magician lurks by the edge of the wall. Under the edge of her cloak I can see several potions she's created to trade with other players. They glint when the light bounces off my armor and hits the glass bottles from a distance.

"I'm looking for some information," I say in a hushed voice as I approach her.

She eyes me skeptically.

"What kind of information could I possibly have?"

"You met with a girl recently—I know you know exactly

whom I mean," I add before she can protest. "I want information."

"She came to me, yes. We traded." A strand of her dark hair slips out from behind her hood. It rests in front of her wrinkled cheek.

"What did you give her?"

She doesn't appear to be too concerned with me so I take another step toward her, trying to intimidate her. I tower over the older woman but it makes no difference.

"She wanted an Acceleration for a new skill. I don't remember which one." She waves her hand as if it's of no consequence.

"You do." She doesn't even flinch when I take another step toward her.

"I do not, young man." She twists to look up at me. "What do you want?"

"Did you do something to her?" I question.

"I didn't," she challenges me, "but it looks like *you* want to."

She pushes past me, knocking against my chest piece. I spin as she moves around me.

"We all got the same message. Go find her yourself," she demands.

"I don't believe you." I dart around her. "What did you do?"

"You think I cursed her?" She glares at me.

"I do."

"I did no such thing, and if you had any experience in

this game, you'd know there's no way for me to do whatever you think I did."

She hurries away from me. I quickly pull up my control panel, trying to check her statistics to see what level she's at but it can't locate her.

"Hey," I rush after her. "What did you do when you gave her the Acceleration?"

"I did nothing," she stoops into a sarcastic bow, "your highness. I gave her the Acceleration she traded me for and she was on her way."

"What did she trade?" I demand.

"Lives, probably. I didn't get to be a magician without understanding the importance of having lives in this game. *You couldn't take me out if you tried.*" She glares at me. "Now run along, *RoyalRoyce*. No one needs you here."

The magician crackles out of the game, evaporating into the air. I wait a moment to make sure it's not a magician's trick, but when she doesn't reappear, I make my way back to Rora.

"Well?" she asks the moment she sees me. She drops the piece of hair she had been nervously twisting while I was gone.

"I think she's in on it. She wouldn't give me any information—acted like she didn't remember your trade—and then pulled out of the game to avoid talking to me," I inform her. "I couldn't even get a read on her statistics. The control panel didn't locate her."

"That's not possible—the control panel *always* picks up

other players' stats." Her eyebrows push down in confusion, scrunching her nose. "What are we supposed to do now?"

"I'm not sure." I'm just as confused as she is. "Let's get closer to the castle and see if there is a higher-level player that can help us. Maybe another magician would know what is going on.

She nods and waits to follow me out of the shadows.

I slip back on to the main part of the street. Rora keeps her hood over her face. It's too bad we can't change our appearances in here without playing as different types of characters—it would be easier to hide Rora if we could change her appearance. We're careful to keep her covered while we walk.

"Royce," Rora suddenly yelps, latching on to my shoulder. Her fingers dig into me—she's stronger than she looks. "That's her."

Rora points over my shoulder toward the castle. The older woman stands there, smiling viciously at us. She cocks one hip out to the side as she straightens, the years melting off her face until she looks young again.

She's the woman from the trading post.

The magician stands there, watching us, a knowing smile on her face. She takes her hand off her hip before spinning around gracefully and walking inside the castle.

Chapter 4

"SHE LEFT THE GAME!" I SHOUT IN CONFUSION.

"*That's* the part you're worried about?" Rora cries behind me. "Her *face* melted off!"

"She's a magician—things happen," I counter.

What I can't figure out is how she could leave the game and then reappear so quickly. I had to wait an entire hour to come back in and help Rora.

"She's not a magician, Royce." Rora corrects me.

Rora steps to the side, spinning me enough to partially face her while still monitoring the castle.

"No magician can do that. And what magician needs to get into the castle for a quest anyway? *Knights* do that. *Royalty* does that. Magicians are playing an entirely different game here. *That over there* doesn't make any sense." She points to the castle dramatically.

The castle glimmers in the sun, reflecting the blue glass color onto the grass in front of it. It twinkles as if glitter has been embedded into its walls. Giant roses sit on vines crawling up the walls, much like on the other buildings, only here there are also blue glass roses resembling the castle embedded on the branches.

The magician is still gone.

"Who is she?" I murmur, still staring.

"Think, Royce," Rora replies. "Who can come and go as they please in that castle?"

"No one," I respond instantly. "No one can come and go in there without having a specific quest to complete."

"Think again," she says calmly, already having figured it out. "Who can come and go as they please? Who can transform at will? Who can keep their statistics from being seen —who can walk around this game cloaked like that? Royce, we're messing with the wrong person."

The only person who has unfettered access to this game is the one that controls the castle—well, that and the game makers but they don't play other than to test new features. They walk around the system like gods that everyone keeps a respectful distance from as they stare in awe. Which leaves only one person—the queen.

"I thought she didn't leave the castle." I squint toward the castle, hoping it offers some new information. It doesn't

"Apparently she does," Rora muses, reaching up to adjust her hood.

"What does she want with you?" I ask.

"I'm in line for the throne, Royce." Her words are simple but it doesn't make them any less complicated.

"What do you mean?" I stammer.

"I'm a threat to her. Technically I could challenge her

claim to the castle at any time. I just haven't." She frowns, green eyes wandering to the ground a few feet away. "I don't want the castle. I just want to play the game."

"You said earlier that—"

"I was proving a point, Royce—I'm better at the game than you. But truthfully, I have no desire for the castle. I just want to beat the dragon, gain more skills, and play the game quietly without any fuss from anyone. But apparently *she* doesn't see it that way."

"So you think that she's trying to make you fail so that you can't take her place."

Rora tucks a strand of hair behind her ear. She struggles a little to avoid knocking off her hood in the process. It's kind of adorable...until she catches me looking.

"What are we supposed to do about this?" I ask, trying to distract her.

"I don't know." She sounds defeated. "The short term goal is to get out of here, but long term...I can't come back if she's going to keep locking me in."

Her eyes fill with tears as she looks up at me. She's nearly a head shorter than me when she hunches down like that—almost like she's deflated.

"Hey," I grab her elbows suddenly to make her face me fully. "We'll find a way to get you home and we'll find a way to get you back into the game safely. Maybe we can make some kind of pact with her."

"You think she's going to let us get close enough?" she asks spitefully. "If I get that close, I could challenge her and that would lock her into the game. I would actually have to defeat her and I don't want that. I just want to play."

"Maybe I could talk to her. She seemed awfully interested in the trading post—"

"You talked to her before?" she snaps, cutting me off.

I suddenly notice the noise swell around us. I glance around, making sure no one has spotted us. When I determine that it was only the natural rise and fall of voices in the game, I look back to her.

"When I was looking for you," I explain. "She came up to me. I brushed her off and went outside where I found you."

"Oh great, *you've* made her mad too."

"Well, to be fair, I think I angered her more just *now* than I did a few hours ago." I give her my best smoldering looking. It doesn't affect her.

This girl is complicated.

"I honestly don't know how you'd get close enough to talk to her at this point," Rora says. "We need to move."

She suddenly swerves from me, walking away from the surge of people crossing the bridge. Her skirt trails out from under her cloak as she walks, making at least two people stop and stare.

"Where are we going?" I ask, jogging to catch up.

"Away from the castle until we can figure out a plan."

"Come on," I say, guiding her onto the bridge. She hesitates for a moment but follows close behind.

Rora keeps her head down as we pass over the wooden bridge to the main part of the game, passing by maidens and knaves trying to trade up on the bridge to the castle. A warlock glances at me but doesn't pay much attention to Rora as she trails behind me.

I've always found it amazing how realistic the textures are inside the game. The harsh boards of the bridge give way to softer, more cushioned grass and dirt as we step back onto the land. The grass shifts in the fake breeze—too bad we can't feel the wind in the game. At least it's temperature controlled.

Without a destination, I navigate us toward the wishing well off to the left. We pass a knight I've been meaning to duel with for the last month but we don't have time for that now, even if I could use the points. I pause, letting Rora inadvertently step up next me, blocking me from his view—it's not worth getting sucked into a battle right now.

I put my hand on her back to keep her moving as she faces me.

"Keep walking," I mumble. She turns back and plays along.

Once we're beyond him, I explain myself, earning a nod.

I'm brought back to reality when my control panel buzzes on my wrist. I nod toward the shade of a giant rock sculpture and we duck behind it.

"What is it?" Rora asks.

"Alan," I reply as I lift the panel to check his message. I try not to frighten her, but sucking in a breath of air quickly probably didn't help my cause.

"Royce?" She says my name like it's a demand—she wants information. Rora latches on to my arm, eyes wild.

"He's been researching," I say, skimming the very short message. We're only allowed a handful of characters per message so Alan can't give me much information. "Oh."

Rora's eyes grow wide and she stretches on to her tiptoes, balancing herself on my arm. Her lips part as if she's going to ask a question but no sound comes out.

"The message is really short but it sounds like we really need to get you out now. He says we have to beat the game."

"But what happens if we don't?" She insists on having an answer. I don't blame her.

I type back to Alan, hoping he can reply quickly. We only get two more messages each before it cuts us off.

I turn my back to the rock as I wait for a reply, leaning against it so I can survey the area. Rora's eyes are locked on me.

"It will be okay," I remind her. If anyone can save her, it's me.

Her jaw tightens as if she doesn't quite believe me. Her breathing moves her shoulder up and down in a restrained repetitive motion—she's concentrating on staying calm.

Alan's next message is more concerning than the first.

"He says he found a man who claims he was locked inside the game. They arrested him for juicing." I glance at her. "We have to beat the game and get you out."

She trembles, realizing her fate if we don't succeed. We don't have much time left before I get taken back out—an hour and half at most. Alan can come back in for an hour and a half after I leave, but Rora might not have that long.

A group of people runs past us, metaphorical and literal pitchforks in hand. They're still chasing her. At least this queen of the castle hasn't raised the price on her head. She must feel incredibly challenged if she's willing to do this to Rora.

"You'll be okay," I insist. "We just have to get you out. What was your next quest? We'll play through and if we have to take on the queen, I'll help you."

"You're willing to give up the game to help me?" she asks cautiously. "I know how seriously you and Alan take this—I checked your stats earlier."

"It's way more important to get you out without causing any damage." I failed to mention that Alan had told me the state of the guy who had been trapped in the game and it wasn't good, but I didn't want to scare her any more than she needed to be. "I can always rebuild. But let's face it, once this queen realizes I'm helping, I probably won't be able to come back to the game anyway."

I shrug casually. In truth, I hate that, but it's better than letting Rora get hurt. She doesn't need to know that now though.

"What's your quest?"

She watches me thoughtfully for a moment, appraising my armor from head to toe. Rora tips her head when she finally reaches my eyes again.

"I have to fight the dragon."

Even *I've* never fought a dragon in this game. It's a fool's errand. Very few people can escape its fire.

I nod.

"Let's go find a dragon."

Unlike dragons from stories, the dragons in the game work on a schedule. They are restricted to certain locations that only higher-level players can enter. Their jobs are to destroy players, sending them back to the beginning of the game.

If you are caught by a dragon without being on a quest to find one, you are eliminated from the game and have to start over from the loest point. If you are vanquished by a dragon while on a quest, you lose all of your lives except for one and have your weapons and skills depleted by half.

If you successfully win in a battle against a dragon, you are advanced to the highest level—the level Rora needs to take on a quest to take the queen's place.

Very few people venture to view the dragons inside the game. Even fewer battle against them.

Still, like clockwork, the dragons announce their presence by sending fiery blasts into the sky, crying out loudly so the kingdom can hear. From what I can tell, there are at least three separate dragons within the game.

From a distance, I've seen at least one black one, but I've heard rumors of red and green dragons as well.

As if they are expecting us, a dragon shrieks somewhere behind the trees. The sound echoes off of nothing—a benefit sound effect of the game—filling their area with a warning not to enter. Rora seems unfazed.

She adjusts her sleeved, then lifts her hands to remove her cloak.

"You're not taking that off, are you?" I question.

"I can't very well fight with that thing on," she replies indignantly, dropping the cloak to the ground. "You don't have to come with me..."

She gives me one last opportunity to back out.

"And miss a dragon fight? Not a chance, princess." I draw my sword, swinging it around in a large loop, hoping to look impressive. "After you, m'lady."

Rora smirks at my antics but doesn't hesitate in walking toward the part of the kingdom that houses the dragons.

"That's her!" someone shouts.

Rora and I look at each other at the same time, rolling our eyes. Here we go again.

She whips around, dagger in hand. I match her with my sword, ready to take on our assailants. A guy attacks me, trying to take me down, but he's distracted watching Rora fight off his friend. I slam into his neck with my blade and he vanishes from the game.

Rora slices at her attacker's arm as he tries to kick her knee out. She leaves a nasty cut followed by a left hook that knocks the guy to the ground, unconscious. He vanishes from the game.

Two more people step up to attack us. When they both launch themselves at Rora, three others decide to rush for me, hoping the winner will share the spoils of defeating Rora with them as a thank you.

I cut one, but not enough to deter him. The tall one slips behind me and attempts to yank my arms behind my back. They scream at their friends to kill Rora.

I go down to my knees as they kick out the back of my legs. My sword tumbles to the ground. The moment I feel the pressure of my knees being kicked out, I prepare myself to toss the man over my back as soon as I hit the ground. He shoots forward, toppling over me as I grab my sword and take out one of the other men.

Rora screams in pain, but it only fuels her. She lashes out at the men in front of her, easily destroying them like it's child's play.

She spins, kicking in the air like a ninja from one of those old movie clips we saw in our history class. Her half skirt spins out behind her in slow motion.

Rora elbows the man in the face, snapping his head back. She spins on her heel, kicking a second man. I charge for him, knocking him to the ground as she takes on the first man.

Both guys disappear at the same time, flickering out of the game. Rora straightens, throwing her shoulders back.

"I hate those guys," she mutters.

"Maybe we need to kill the kill order first," I suggest.

"We don't have time. Most of them can't get into the restricted zone anyway. Let's just go find a dragon."

"If you're sure…"

"I am. Let's go." She turns and marches toward the invisible wall that the newer players can't cross.

The wall tingles as we pass through it, letting us know we are in a different zone. Several people who were part of the hunting pack run up to us, bouncing off the wall when they don't realize they can't enter. I'd laugh at the look of shock on their faces when I turn around after hearing the slam, but we don't have time for that.

"Can you pull up any information on the dragons?" I inquire, hoping to find some sort of advantage.

"I don't know, but I think we should walk a little deeper into the bushes and take cover before I check. I think we need to be hyper vigilant now that we're here," Rora points out.

We walk deeper into the overgrown area that becomes so thick that it's like we're walking through a jungle. It wouldn't surprise me if we walked right by a dragon hiding under the foliage and had no idea.

"Here," Rora finally says, stepping into the shelter of a large tree-like structure that's so covered with trees we have to move branches back like we're swimming in the ocean.

After a moment, we come to a small opening, big enough to fit both of us without being poked by branches.

Rora puts her back against a tree trunk, preparing to search her control panel for information. She glances up, catching me staring again. Dang, she's pretty.

"Should you maybe," she pauses, hoping I'll catch on. When I don't, she continues, "watch the area for threats?"

She looks at me like I'm clueless.

"Right," I spin, realizing I'm acting like an idiot.

My eyes scan the area for signs of danger. Each shift of the leaves on the tree catches my attention as I listen carefully. I could use some coffee right now.

"It looks like there are five dragons here. If one engages with me, I have to fight it, but there are some that are easier to defeat than the others."

"Which ones are those?" I quickly ask.

"Navy," she replies, still staring at her control panel. "The problem is that it's hard to tell the difference between the navy and the black dragon since they're so similar in coloring and shape. Black is the deadliest."

"Perfect, we could either run into the easiest or toughest dragon and have to battle it because we don't know which one it is."

"Exactly." Her eyes never flicker from her screen.

"Okay, so what's the second easiest? I say we go after that one."

"Green can spit fire like the rest of them, but it also cause hurricane-like windstorms with its wings."

She finally looks up at me. Ah, so that thing in my stomach is a windstorm that her green eyes are creating. *Makes sense.*

"That's the second easiest to defeat?"

She nods miserably.

"Okay, so we go find the green dragon and make sure we don't get treated like kites."

"How? You want to tie ourselves down? We can't fight that way," she protests.

It's an interesting thought, but somehow I can't imagine attaching ourselves to boulders with chains is going to do any good.

"I don't suppose I could tame it," she muses.

"I sincerely doubt that," I reply, making her frown, despite her eyes sparkling.

"Well, prince charming, *you* try coming up with an idea," she snaps.

"Prince charming?" I scoff.

"Your screen name is RoyalRoyce, what do you expect me to say?"

"Personally, I'd go with *king* over prince, but whatever," I grin, flexing my muscles under my armor. She makes a face. I'm starting to like her more and more...but there would be time to flirt with her later.

We both fall to the ground when an earth-shattering scream rings out over our heads.

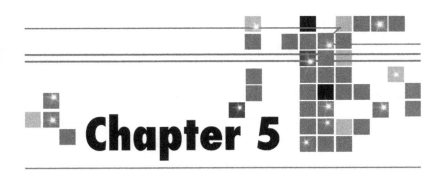

Chapter 5

A GUST OF WIND KNOCKS THE TREES FROM AROUND US, exposing us to the open sky. A dragon darts out of view.

"Which one was it?" Rora shrieks over the noise.

"I don't know—it was too dark to tell!" I yell back, trying to crawl to her. "That's an insane amount of wind though, so maybe it's our green dragon?"

"We need a better look." Rora says, standing. Now that the dragon is out of sight, the trees right themselves, stretching back up to their normal height. "I'm climbing up."

Before I can stop her, she scales the tree she was leaning against as if it was nothing. I'd have to remember to get the Stickiness modification next time I was in the Mod shop. It's clearly an epic thing to spend my credits on.

Rora stands on a branch high above my head. Now I see why she opted for pants with a half skirt—that wouldn't be nearly as easy in a full dress like some of the girls wear in the game. She spins quickly in a circle as she searches for the dragon.

It appears out of nowhere, suddenly filling the space

with another gust of wind. Rora clutches at the trunk of the tree, trying to balance herself.

The dragon shrieks, shaking the ground under my feet. The beast tips its head up, releasing fire into the sky—right on time. Smoke trails from its mouth for a moment as it looks back down.

Rora topples from the tree, unable to catch herself. I rush forward, trying to reach her. She slams into my arms, elbow knocking painfully into my shoulder. I cringe as I nearly drop her.

She bounces in my arms trying to catch herself against me. When her hair smacks against my face, I get the most incredible scent of her shampoo. It smells like roses.

Rora flips herself out of my arms before I can register the pain of our collision.

"Bad news," she yelps. "It's the black dragon."

I look up, horrified.

"How do you know?"

"That little reappearing act that it just pulled—not an act. It can actually disappear and reappear," she warns me.

As she speaks the words, the dragon vanishes, leaving only the rush of wind from its wings behind as a reminder of its presence.

"We have to run," she gasps, turning to me. "We need to stay on the move."

Rora grabs at my hand, forcing me into action. The world stills as we run, crashing through the brush, but the light suddenly changes from the pure white light of day inside the game to a vibrant golden tone.

The dragon has reappeared and cut off our path with a trail of fire. The tall, dark monster creeps along the ground, strategically placing its feet to move in a way that would intimidate anyone.

He eyes us before hissing loudly.

"I see you've met my pet," a voice rings out. "When one defeats a dragon, the rest of them bend to your will, *word to the wise.*"

The raven-haired woman walks around from behind the dragon, petting it on the nose. She's changed into a red medieval gown with sleeves that nearly reach the grass. Must be nice to be the queen and do whatever you want.

"Why are you doing this to me?" Rora confronts the woman.

"Why else, dear? You're getting too close."

"I don't want your castle," Rora challenges. "I have no desire to take your place. I just wanted to play the game. Let me go home and I won't come back."

"Nice try, princess. No one works as hard as you did just to give up when they're so close to ruling." She swings her hip to the side like she had done in front of the castle. "But you're right about one thing—you won't be coming back."

My stomach drops. I should have told her.

"You see, RoraRose, while you're locked in here, your body isn't doing so well out there. If you die this time in the game, the game takes it out on your body," the woman informs her. "The last one didn't fair so well, I hear."

She grins as she takes a step toward us. I fight the urge to sweep Rora behind my back. Inside the game, my strength is no different than her strength, but her skills are better because she's higher ranking. While she can handle herself, if I take the game-death first, that gives her at least one more chance to save herself. I just have to time it correctly, and now is not that time.

Rora matches the woman, stepping forward. The dragon turns to her, watching. One snap of its jaws and it wouldn't even have to use its fire on Rora.

She surveys it, hand lingering near her dagger. That little thing won't be enough against the magician queen.

"Who are you?" Rora challenges her.

The woman waves her hand in the air. Our control panels buzz on our wrists—she unlocked her information.

"MaraAdrielle, Kingdom Queen," Rora reads.

"I've ranked higher than you'll ever rank, little girl," Mara glares at her. "No one else has even come close. It will be a shame to see you go though."

"I thought there was someone else that wasn't doing well," Rora reminds her. Vindication is written on her face.

"He reached a level where I decided he was a threat, but to *your* credit, he wasn't as good as you." She sneers at Rora. The two are locked in conversation as if I'm not even there —maybe I can use that to my advantage.

"So what's your plan here? Have your dragon eat me?" Rora tips her chin up defiantly.

"That's too pedestrian. Anyone could have their dragon roast you," she leers at Rora as she starts to circle her. "No, I think I'll have Drayce destroy your *boyfriend* instead."

Mara throws herself sideways, evading her dragon's wing as it wheels around to face me. It roars in my face as it begins to run toward me. Thankfully I'm close enough that it can't gain much speed in the distance between us.

I manage to grab on to the hilt of my sword, holding the blade in front of me, as the monster runs at me. Rora shrieks, trying to draw the dragon's attention away.

"Remember, RoraRose," Mara calls to her, "if he dies, there's no coming back for him—he's not supposed to be here. He may have other lives, but he's starting from the bottom. He can't help you if he's dead."

She laughs as the dragon's eyes grow wild. From the corner of my eye, I see Rora run toward the dragon, trying to defend me and draw its attention away long enough for me to stab it.

Rora throws herself against its leg, driving her dagger into its scaly flesh. Just as I thrust my sword upward into its heart, it disappears.

"Did we do it?" I call to Rora.

"Hardly," Mara chirps. She snaps her fingers and the dragon reappears on her other side, decidedly far away from Rora. "But if you're not a fan of Drayce here, I can always call Ejder."

Above our heads, the sound of swopping fills the air. The dragon's flame shoots high above it, letting the kingdom know it is here. When he settles on the ground, I find he matches Mara's deep red dress. I wonder if she borrowed some of its scales for her belt.

The red dragon moves its tail as it sizes me up.

"What does this one do?" I say just loud enough for Rora to hear me. I keep my lips from moving as much as possible.

"It's resistant to weapons." She looks like she's ready to be sick.

"What?" I nearly drop my sword, turning to look at her. I probably shouldn't have done that.

"We can't use weapons on it," she repeats. "We can hurt it a little, but we can't do any serious damage and we can't kill it."

"How do we—?"

"Without weapons," she cuts me off.

"And you said the *other one* is hardest to kill?" My voice goes up an octave but I don't care.

"Last chance, pretty thing. Leave now and I'll spare you. It's only *her* that I want...in fact, if you leave now, I'll let you into the castle for a quest. You can score unfathomable points and lives inside. And if you work with me, there won't ever be a need for me to do *this* to *you*." Mara waves her hand around at the scene. Her dragons surround us, forcing us back with their tails.

"You can't use both dragons on us," Rora calls, fully prepared to take on the black dragon advancing on her. "My quest only calls for one dragon to be slain. Once I engage with one, the other can't attack."

"That won't stop the other from going after your boyfriend," Mara cackles. "Unless, of course, he makes a wiser choice."

She holds her hand out to me. The wind from her dragon's wings pushes her hair back like it would in one of those movie sequences. She's actually quite stunning for a moment.

"Nah, I'm a loyal boyfriend," I call, making her face falter. "I also know that once I'm engaged with a dragon, a second one can't attack me."

Knowing Rora had no idea I would be saying that out loud to Mara, I launch myself toward her. It would have been better if we could have both taken the red dragon together, but Rora didn't know my plan until I announced it to both women.

The red dragon—Ejder— reels back as if he's been slapped. I've confused him. His jaw snaps open and shut once before making his move.

I dive to the ground, rolling over to get out of the way as his flames tingle across my skin. Despite the suit of armor, I can feel the fire licking at my arm, singeing the hair like a fireplace I once got too close to as a child.

When I stand, I'm by Rora's side. She glances at me to make sure I'm okay before lashing out at the black dragon. I slice at it with her, locking both of us in battle with the creature.

"Ejder, come," Mara commands. The red dragon recoils, wallowing in misery at its failed attempt to destroy me. I can't hide my grin at evading it, though the black dragon's roar removes it completely.

Mara leans against her red dragon, getting cozy to watch the show. It wraps itself around her, protecting her.

"Come here, my pet. Let's watch your brother defeat the little knight and his princess," Mara croons loudly enough for us to hear. "Drayce will do a magnificent job destroying them. Drayce, darling...*kill the knight first.*"

The black dragon's head whips away from Rora. It screeches a loud war cry, tipping his head back to release his fire into the air above us.

Rora uses the opportunity to bring her dagger down on the dragon's toe, slicing it off. Drayce comes down in pain, shrieking and shaking its head. Eyes narrow as Rora and the dragon face off.

I race toward the beast, angling my sword to enter its heart. I'm positive there's no way it will be this easy, but I'm willing to try. I have the overwhelming urge to yell my own battle cry as I run, but alerting the monster probably isn't a good idea.

It sees me despite my best efforts and picks up his foot, slamming it into my body. Drayce tosses me like a rag doll. I roll as I hit the ground, losing my sword in the process.

The red dragon hisses at me as I sit up. It's nostrils flare as it looks at me with pure hatred.

"Shame," Mara mouths to me, petting her dragon. She smiles and shrugs before looking at Rora.

I jump to my feet, running toward Rora and the black dragon. When I finally locate my sword, it's in Rora's hands. She wields it against the dragon ferociously.

"I'm here," I shout, trying not to throw her off her game.

"Grab the bow," she instructs, angling her back to me.

"Already on it," I reply, surprised we were thinking the same thing.

I haven't used a bow inside the game very often, but I have used them in real life—*thank you, physical education mandates*—so I imagine it will be fairly similar.

It feels steady in my hands as I knock an arrow and aim toward the digital dragon's eye. I might not kill it, but I can blind it and give Rora every chance possible.

Smoke streams from the dragon's nostrils as my arrow finds its mark. A low, guttural sound emanates from its closed jaws.

"Don't stop," Rora demands.

I stay by her side, pulling arrows from the quiver strapped to her back. Our legs and hips find a place next to each other, as if we share a side like conjoined twins. When she moves, I move.

"You okay?" she asks, clearly out of breath.

"Fine, you?" I reply. I haven't done as much lunging as she has because my weapon is long distance while hers is for close range attacks. "Ready to switch?"

"Not sure we have time for that," she mutters.

"Have any other tricks up your sleeve, princess?"

When I glance around, I notice the underbrush has fallen away, leaving the entire area to look like a peaceful meadow—there's nowhere for us to hide even if we *do* get away. I didn't realize the game changed landscapes in this section of the kingdom.

"One, but it might get us killed in the process," she says. Her arms sink as if she's growing tired from holding the heavy metal sword. "We could blow it up."

The dragon disappears in front of us. I quickly flip around to face the other direction, watching our backs. I knock an arrow and wait.

"Define *blowing it up*," I request.

The red dragon screeches as if cheering its brother on.

"I have the ability to create an explosion, but if we don't get out of the way fast enough, it could take us down too.

Drayce reappears to my left, warning us with the loud stomping of its feet. It crouches low, slowly moving toward us. Rora and I turn to face it, putting me on her right side— exactly where I don't want to be.

It breathes fire at us, glittering flames bursting in our faces. Before it hits us, Rora tosses her arms up, throwing an invisible shield in front of us. The flames hit it, bouncing off of the shield back toward it.

"One time use, sorry," she explains why she hadn't used it earlier.

The dragon frowns—something I didn't realize digital dragons could do—and takes another step toward us.

"So," I try to say casually, "are we blowing this monster up, or what?"

"It takes time to prepare, Royce. Can you hold him off while I get it ready?" She sounds nervous. I've been willing to help with everything else, so why not this?

"I've got this," I say, picking up my sword from where Rora had dropped it on the ground to summon her shield.

Rora falls back. I glance over my shoulder to see where she is so I keep the dragon away from her and catch Mara leaning forward with a concerned look on her face. I hope we accidentally blow her up too, though I imagine as queen, she can't die in the game until someone takes her place inside the castle—I haven't bothered to learn the rules for taking over as head royalty in the castle yet since I still have a few levels to go.

Drayce and I face off. It circles around me, trying to cut me off from Rora, but I hold my ground. I won't give it the advantage.

The dragon rears up, crashing down next to me as it coils its tail around me. I slam the point of my sword into its scales as it lifts me off the ground.

"Royce!" Rora calls from somewhere behind the dragon. I catch the tiniest glimpse of her blonde hair and purple collar as the dragon shakes me, trying to remove the sword from its flesh.

Mara pushes away from the red dragon and glides quickly toward Rora.

"You can't interfere while I'm on a quest!" Rora shouts.

Inside the game, once a person is locked in a battle quest, no one can interfere unless they started the quest at the same time. *I* have the ability to mess up Rora's plans but *Mara* can't do anything but wait until the battle is finished since she didn't engage in the battle at the same time.

The queen waits restlessly for the battle to finish. If she has it her way, the fight will end with both Rora and I being removed from the game. If Rora loses, I can never come back even if the game allows me to start over.

I pull a dagger from the belt around my waist, driving it into the dragon's tail at the same time I pull the sword out. It wasn't expecting the attack and drops me, disappearing.

Avoiding my sword while I fall, I plummet fifteen feet, crashing into the ground.

"Royce!" Rora shouts again. I can't say I hate it when she says my name.

"I'm okay," I grunt, picking myself back up.

"Where is it?" she demands, rushing toward me. She carefully holds her explosive device under the open front hem of the skirt near her hip.

"It will be back," I promise.

"When it returns, get out of my way. Get as far away from here as you can. I have speed that I can unlock to get away, so don't wait for me," she instructs me.

"Got it," I confirm just as the dragon reappears in front of us. It glares at us harder than Mara has been.

"Get your sword up like you're going to fight, then wait for me to throw the device," Rora mumbles.

I glance down, looking around her body to the hand she's attempting to keep concealed with her half skirt. She's angled toward me, blocking the dragon from noticing the gold and jewel-encrusted circle she's holding. It could pass as a dragon egg if it were a bit larger.

Something clicks.

She locks eyes with me, nodding. We both take a step forward as if to charge at the beast. It rears up, preparing to take us on, but only Rora steps forward.

Rora throws the gold device at the dragon and it skitters under its body. The moment she releases it, I run, looking back over my shoulder.

The dragon lets out a vicious cry of terror, it's red sibling echoing its concern. Mara screams as Rora starts to run.

I pump my legs as fast as I can, propelling myself forward. Rora quickly catches up to me, grabbing my elbow as she forces me to run faster, lending me part of her strength.

A single rock stands in the middle of the meadow, having shifted to give us a place to hide from the explosion. We dive behind it.

Rora trips as we hide behind the rock. I grab at her, trying to steady her, but I end up falling on top of her. I cover my head with my hands to protect myself from debris. She wraps herself around me, trying to help protect me while I act as a human shield for her.

The detonation is so loud, I'm positive the entire

kingdom can hear it. I picture the knaves and warlocks all jerking around to face this forbidden part of the kingdom, wondering what is going on.

Digital debris floats down from the sky as if pieces of the blue above us were drifting down. In fact, pixels from the dragon are mixed with pixels from the sky and grass. They twist and loop as they settle around us, disappearing once they hit the grass.

I pull away from Rora quickly, allowing us both to look out from behind the rock. Mara marches toward us with her dragon in tow.

"You may have beat the quest, RoraRose, but you won't be able to take my throne. I'll see to it that you never escape in one piece."

Mara waves her hand, disappearing as she shatters into a millions glitch-filled pieces.

The red dragon hisses at us, shooting flames straight up into the air over its head. It lifts itself off the ground and flies toward the castle, breaking the barrier that limits where dragons can roam.

In the distance, it settles onto the high walls of the crystal castle, waiting for us to approach. It roars, daring us to come to the final battle for the title of queen.

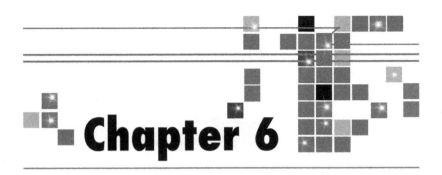

Chapter 6

"I GUESS WE'RE GOING TO THE CASTLE," I MUTTER, SIGHING dramatically. "Are you injured?"

"I'm fine," she says, refusing to look at me.

"You healed yourself, didn't you?" I ask. I need to know how badly she depleted her options.

She nods miserably.

"How bad?"

"Pretty bad. There's not much left."

Her hair has fallen out of its swept up look, making her look like she's been through battle. Dirt covers her face and I can only imagine how I look.

"You need to do whatever you have to in order to survive. Don't be discouraged. Now all we have to do is take Mara down." I give her a confident smile.

"Do you have any idea who she is?" Rora asks as she starts walking toward the castle.

"Not a clue. I don't think I've ever seen her before today."

"Too bad, we could really use some leverage on her."

"Wait." I pause. "I still have a few messages with Alan. Let me ask him to look her up. I type quickly on my control panel, asking for information on the magician queen. Hopefully he'll respond soon.

"At least we took the dragon out. Great thinking on your part," I offer as we start walking again.

"Thanks. I've been storing that one for awhile."

"It was a good call," I affirm. "Hey, you know once we walk out of here, the kill challenge will still be in effect."

"Yeah, we'll have to avoid that." She taps the quiver on her back, replenished with new arrows.

"Do we have a plan for that?"

The grass ripples in the nonexistent breeze. Rora tucks a strand of her curly hair behind her ear.

"Fight them off, I guess. We don't have much choice at this point."

My control panel buzzes as she finishes speaking.

"What does he say?"

I pull up the message.

"Her sister is one of the game's creators," I read out loud. "Mara was banned from playing the game when it was new because her family didn't like the idea of immersive virtual reality, so she snuck in under an alias and went on to level really high."

I close my control panel over, looking at Rora.

"It sounds like there's a division between them. Alan is trying to get in contact with the one game maker now. I have a feeling she'll help us to oust her sister from the game."

"Well, that would certainly help."

The red dragon screeches in the distance, clearly annoyed that we are taking so long. It spits fire over the bridge making everyone duck. The curious people that stayed to investigate the dragon's appearance at the castle clear out of the area quickly.

"Huh. Guess that will make the kill challenge easier to avoid," I muse.

"Looks like it," she says, working her hair back up into its sweeping up do. I suppose she can't fight with hair in her eyes. "Maybe we should pick up the pace. I can't stand drawing this out any longer."

I match her speed as we run toward the castle.

"Do you think we'll have to fight to get inside?" I ask, staring at the red dragon. It watches us walk across the second bridge. I doubt dousing it in the moat would drown it, but maybe it would extinguish the fire.

The dragon hisses at us, clawing at the top of a tower. Crystal blue bricks fall off the building, smashing like glass when it hits the courtyard ground.

"Pretty sure," she surmises.

The dragon's tail swishes down in front of the castle

door as it opens revealing Mara on the other side. She's changed outfits again, this time standing in her own version of armor.

Dark metal surrounds her body, dripping over her like pointed dragon scales. Each one moves individually as she steps out of the castle.

"Congratulations, RoraRose," she says as if mandated to speak the words. "To make it this far is quite the accomplishment. You now have a choice—battle me for the throne or leave the game."

"I choose to leave the game," Rora shouts immediately.

Mara's shoulders drop.

"Oh, you stupid girl," she shouts. "You don't *really* have a choice—I locked you in, remember? The game just requires me to say that."

Mara walks closer, each step more dangerous than the last.

"To win against me, you must enter the castle and succeed in taking my power. Only one of us can win and neither of us can leave until someone is declared the victor by the game." Mara turns to me. "*He* can't come inside. You might want to kiss your prince good bye now, RoraRose, because before I'll let you enter my castle, *I'm going to kill him.*"

She throws her hand to the side, a bolt of something flying out from her fingertips. It strikes the ground at my feet, burning a hole into the otherwise perfect grass. Mara smiles wickedly.

"You had your chance," she taunts.

Rora rushes to stand in front of me.

"You can't hurt me while I'm out here." She wraps her arms around me as I stand behind her. Her fingers graze my back as she presses herself against my chest, her quiver nearly poking me in the face.

"No, but I *can* move you out of the way." She raises her hand as if she's going to snap for her dragon.

As I watch her, I wonder how she's going to fight with half her hair tucked up like that. It's like it's pulled back and up on one half of her head while the other half hangs loose and bold. She tosses part of it while watching us.

Rora fidgets behind me as if she's trying to type into her control panel on her wrist. I wind my hands in front of her, trying to give her more room to work without Mara noticing her movements.

I glare at the queen, hoping to hold her attention.

"You can't touch me," I challenge her. "Not in the trading post and certainly not here."

"You'll see soon enough that power is attractive, Royal-Royce. You wanted this too. Don't deny it—you've been working toward this moment for *yourself* for all of these years. Even if your little princess *does* beat me, you'll be battling *her* within a few months. Isn't it nice to have already learned all of her tricks?"

Something zaps inside of me. Rora transferred something to me. It registers in my control panel but I can't check it yet.

"Oh, trust me, I've only just begun learning her tricks. She and I have a lot more to teach each other." *Hopefully outside of the game too.* "Don't worry, Mara, we won't even think about you once when you're gone."

Mara grimaces, baring her teeth.

"We'll see about that." She takes a deep breath, preparing to launch her dragon attack.

My hands find their way to Rora's hips, ready to push her aside if I need to. The dragon can't kill her at this point, but he can still injure her enough that she can't defend herself once she's inside the castle walls.

"Pity, that handsome face could have been such a nice addition to my throne room. Maybe I'll stuff your avatar once Ejder destroys you— *assuming* he doesn't burn your face off—and set you up in the castle anyway. You could be my muse."

Rora works one arm around me, placing it between her back and my chest so it's resting on my opposite hip. She's preparing to push me into action. I wait for her signal.

"Well, then, here's hoping it burns me to a crisp," I shout.

Her hand claws at my hip, forcing me to step to the side of her.

"Stickiness," she hisses. "Go!"

I run for the castle, surprising Mara. She spins as I dart past her and leap onto the wall of the castle. I gracefully scale it.

If this ability doesn't stick around after this level, I'm going to do whatever it takes to get it back—it's incredible.

The dragon shakes its head as it watches me climb, shocked to see me move like that. Behind me, I can hear Rora engage with Mara, distracting her.

I jump for the dragon before it can react, slicing off part of its tail. I wish my weapons could do more damage. It wails in pain, sending more crystal bricks shattering to the ground. I fall among the glass pieces.

The dragon whips around to face Mara, realizing she's fighting. It throws itself away from the castle wall, landing near its mistress.

Knowing it can hurt Rora, and being fully aware that Rora only has one chance to escape, I know what I must do.

With sword in hand, I take on the dragon that cannot be killed with weapons.

I won't be coming out of this alive.

"Rora, get inside!" I insist, holding my blade above my shoulder.

"I'm not leaving you," she refuses. "We're in this together."

"No, Rora, we're not. You can only win if you get inside and fight that witch. I can't go in either way, but if you defeat her, you can call off the dragon! Now, go!"

Fire races through the air toward me, sizzling against my armor. It warms enough to burn through the metal as it touches my skin. I cry out, dropping my sword.

Rora looks like she wants to cry, but my words ring true —she's the one that has the power to stop this.

"Go!" I beg her, stooping to pick up my weapon.

She looks at Mara. The queen has her hands buried in Rora's hair, trying to pull it. Rora's hands are piercing into the queen's shoulders, her arms locked to keep her at a distance.

Rora growls at her, sounding for a moment like a dragon. She digs her nails into Mara's arms and forces her toward the opaque glass building.

"Give up, child," Mara yelps. "You don't have the power to defeat me. I will always rule this kingdom."

"You mean your *sister's* kingdom?" Rora defies her.

"She may have built this world, but *I* own it."

The dragon snaps at me, swiping at me with its tail at the same time. I drop to my knees as it pulls my leg out from under me. Heat radiates off of the creature.

"Not for long," Rora challenges.

"I've been at this much longer than you have, *princess*. I watched this game take over my sister's life—I know every trick about it."

"So when she wouldn't let you play, you thought the best revenge of all would be mastering her game?" Rora shouts, taunting her. The two grapple, clawing at each other. Rora's dagger bounces off the queen like it's nothing since they can't hurt each other until they are inside.

The dragon lifts me up, flying back to the nearest tower of the castle. My hand still sticks to the walls, giving me at least some hope.

I can hear the woman shouting, but from high on the castle walls, I can't make out the words. From the look on

Mara's face as she swings them around, I'd guess Rora is roasting her about her sister.

The dragon moves me from its tail to its clawed front foot, lifting me up as if it's going to eat me. Its teeth are large and stained black, nearly the size of my forearm and hand.

I slap it as it leans into me. It shakes its head, allowing me to get a good punch to the nose. My fingers claw at it, trying to defend myself. Rora needs to get moving.

"Royce!" she shouts.

"*Royce!*" Mara mimics. "Ah, young love. Too bad it never lasts."

"Let him go, Mara," Rora demands. "He can be your little pet."

Her negotiating tactics are lacking.

"Bring him here, Ejder," Mara summons, breaking away from Rora.

The red dragon lifts into the air, dropping on the grass with me still in its clutches. I bring a brick with me that it loosened when the dragon landed on the edge of the wall. It doesn't notice as I hide it behind my back.

When we're settled, Mara walks over to us. Only Rora's nails digging into her arm stops her from getting too close.

"Kill him," Mara commands.

"This ends now," Rora summons all of her strength, dragging the woman toward the castle. She calls out to me, "I'll be back, Royce."

The dragon turns to me and I strike. The glass causes

enough damage to get the beast to release me. I drop to the ground, readying my sword.

I know Rora's watching behind me as she hurries toward the castle so I shout goodbye to her.

"I'll be fine—*just get out*! I'll see you outside!"

Fire surrounds me, melting my skin, as I plunge my sword into the dragon's heart.

I fade out of the game as the castle door slams shut.

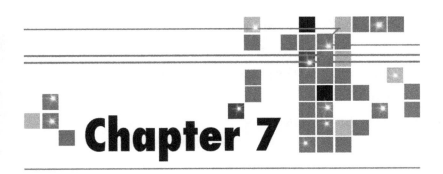

Chapter 7

I WAKE WITH A START.

"Royce!" Alan shouts, racing across the room. "Where is she?"

"She had to defeat Mara alone," I glance up to see Perry rushing at me. "Aunt Perry?"

"It was either get her out of here or watch you two. I couldn't stop her," Alan informs me. "Chrystal said not to leave Rora alone."

"Who is Chrystal?"

"She's the game creator, dear," Perry says nervously as she fusses over me. "She's supposed to be hacking into the system to help Rora escape.

"Supposed to be?" I demand, swinging my feet over the edge of the chair.

"She *is*," Alan corrects. "Perry is just being paranoid."

"We can't let her die, Royce," Perry begs.

"She won't die. I've been with her for hours. She's got the skills to beat Mara."

"Why did you leave her?" Perry demands, grabbing my shoulder. I shake her off.

"I had to die in the game so she could defeat Mara."

"Dude, you died?" Alan asks. He sounds a little sad. We won't be able to play together for a long time until I reach higher levels again. "At least you protected her."

His ability to bounce back is astounding.

I maneuver myself to stand next to Rora.

"She's not moving," I frown.

"Perry, Royce needs coffee. He's had a long few hours and if we're going to help Rora, he needs to be thinking clearly." He waits as Perry rushes downstairs as if our lives depended on it. He's somber when he speaks again. "She hasn't moved for the last twenty minutes. I'm really worried."

It takes a great deal of effort to lift Rora's fingers off the armrest, but I slip my hand under hers.

"Dude, what happened to you?" Alan asks as I swallow hard. "You've only been in there for a few hours and you look like you're losing your best friend—which, by the way, is supposed to be *me*."

"We can't let her get hurt in there, Alan. She doesn't deserve this." I can't take my eyes off her. It doesn't even look like she's breathing. "When was the last time you were in contact with Chrystal?"

"A little while ago. She was still hacking in. She's trying to circumvent the system because it was design so that people couldn't hijack it. She knew her sister had snuck into the game and taken the castle but she didn't know she was hurting people on the outside to keep it."

"She didn't know about that guy Mara got locked up for juicing?" I question.

Wait, did Rora blink? No? No.

My shoulders sag when I realize it was wishful thinking.

"Turns out Mara has some clout out here. She's a judge. She had the records sealed and refused to let the media report on it. That's why I only found it on that one website. It took some serious digging, let me tell you." He raises an eyebrow at me. "Oh, and her real name isn't Mara. It's Dara. She changed it for the game."

"A judge…wow."

"Here," Perry runs into the room, thrusting a cup of coffee at me. It sloshes on the floor, this time avoiding my hand.

"Thanks," I take a quick sip and hand it to Alan to set down, unwilling to move away from Rora.

The girl in the chair gasps, making us all leap into the air. Aside from that, she doesn't move.

The waiting takes forever. Alan paces around the room, sending Perry on a thousand little missions to get her out of our hair.

"Should I go in there?" Alan asks.

"No, she's in the castle. You can't do anything to help her."

"Should I contact Chrystal again?" Alan has been known to babble when he gets anxious.

"We might hurt Rora's chances if we bother Chrystal and distract her."

I'm trying to think practically about this.

If I weren't attached to Rora's hand, I'd be pacing around the room too, likely lapping Alan despite how fast he's walking. I lean against the chair's armrest with one elbow, holding her hand in the other, willing her to make *some* movement.

Alan rounds the corner again.

"We just turned into a trio, didn't we?" He offers me a sad smile.

"Yeah, I think we did," I reply, glancing down. We'd known this girl for a handful of hours and already she was one of us.

"Her mother is going to kill me," Perry cries from the doorway.

"Out!" we both shout at her, making her retreat.

"Go handle her," I direct Alan, feeling terrible for yelling at my aunt.

Alan swiftly walks out of the room, guiding Perry down the stairs. He'll drop her on the couch, calm her down, and be right back up.

Rora rests in the chair, her hair curled in ringlets around her shoulders. I move a strand away from her lips.

"I just need you to wake up, Rora. Come on, you can do it. You can defeat her," I whisper, knowing she can't hear me.

Alan's phone lights up, buzzing.

I let go of Rora for the first time and run across the room, snatching it up.

"Hello," I answer.

"Who is this?" a female voice yelps.

"Alan's friend, Royce."

"Oh," she says. "This is Chrystal. You're out of the game?"

"I died," I answer bluntly.

"Are you with her?"

"Yes." I rush back to her side.

"Good, it's nearly over," her voice rises in pitch as she rushes to get in her words. "You're going to hear static, when you do, take the goggles off of her and then don't touch it. Stay on the line."

The end of her words are overtaken by a loud crackling sound as if our entire gaming system in the room is about to combust. I drop the phone on Rora's leg as I quickly remove the goggles. Her hair falls out of place, dangling off the sides of the headrest.

"Royce? Royce?" the voice on the phone asks. I jerk my head around to locate the device.

"I'm here," I yelp as the phone collides with my ear.

"What is she doing?" Chrystal asks.

"Royce?" Perry shouts up the stairs, having heard the noise.

Alan and Perry pound up the stairs.

"Nothing," I answer.

Rora sits there. She's not moving, she's not breathing, she's not doing anything.

"Don't touch her. Just wait," Chrystal cautions.

The two on the stairs are getting closer. They try to launch themselves in the door but I hold up a hand to stop them. Alan slams his palms into the side of the doorway as Perry collides with his back. He stops her from entering. She fights to peer around him.

"Wait," I whisper, directing them to stay outside.

It seems like an eternity passes.

"She's not moving," I gulp into the phone finally.

"Try to call her awake," Chrystal says. She doesn't sound like she thinks it will work.

"Rora?" I watch her closely. "Rora."

I can't tell if her chest rises with a breath or not. I might be making the movement up.

"Rora, please open your eyes," I try again. "Rora, please."

Her lips part slightly, the first sign of life. Rora's eyelashes, long and dark with her makeup, start to tremble.

It takes time, but she finally opens her eyes.

"Royce," she croaks.

Alan rushes in, grabbing my coffee that has now cooled. He hands it to me and I hold it to Rora's lips. The liquid clears her throat, giving her the ability to speak.

"Keep her down, Royce." Chrystal says through the phone. "I'm on my way."

"Stay down, you'll be okay." I gently push Rora's shoulder back. "Are you all right?"

She takes a deep breath. Rora looks over herself, moving her fingers and toes, checking for any injuries. So far, she seems to have returned in the same condition that she left.

"I'm okay," she replies cautiously. She tries to sit up quickly, but I catch her. "You died."

"It's okay. I'm fine," I insist. Perry stifles her sniffing in the background as Alan corrals her to the door.

"What happened in there?" I ask.

"I dragged Mara into the castle. I was winning, believe it or not. Then, right before I fizzled out, something happened. It was like the entire game was glitching. I think the entire kingdom got kicked out of the game."

"That was probably Mara's sister," I inform her.

"Royce...I won," she announces.

"You won?" I repeat.

"*You won?*" Alan shouts excitedly. "You *won!*"

"You won!" I grin at her. "*You're* the queen."

"I'm the queen," she says softly, grinning back at me.

"Well, congratulations, your majesty." Alan bows from the doorway, still holding back Perry.

"I'm okay, Perry," Rora insists.

Perry breaks down in tears. Alan rolls his eyes at us and helps her back down the stairs to the couch. It would be much easier if she just stayed there.

"*Godmothers*, right?" Rora jokes. She pauses, looking back at me quietly. "But the good news is, I'm queen now."

A playful grin tugs at the corner of her lips.

"Yes you are," I grin back, leaning toward her. I'd happily kiss her right now, but it's probably too soon, so I hold off.

She rolls her eyes when I don't get her implied point.

"And as queen, I control certain aspects of the game, Royce."

"Congratulations," I tease, giving her my best smoldering grin.

"Congratulations to *you*," she says softly, hand pushing my chest back. "I've restored you to the game. Turns out that I get to do a lot of fun things now."

"I'm back in the game?" I gasp. I didn't even know that was possible.

"Back in the game and up two levels for your bravery while helping me." She settles back into the chair, leaning into her hair as it rests on the chair flirtatiously. Her hand brushes against my wrist. "Thanks for your help in there, Royce."

"We make a great team, your highness."

"Stop calling me that," she smirks at me.

"No, I don't think I will," I tease. "I'm glad you're awake, Rora."

"Me too. At least I had my two knights to help me. Speaking of which, I should probably promote Alan too so it doesn't look like I'm playing favorites, huh?"

"Probably," I agree. "But we all know I'm your favorite."

"Whatever," she rolls her eyes, back to acting the girl I met outside the trading post.

"Back to *this*, are we?" I gesture between us.

"You didn't honestly think saving me was going to change anything, did you? Nice try," she says sarcastically.

"Your name might call you *royal* but there's only room for one princess here and that's me, *peasant*."

Funny enough, I'd serve in her court any day. Learning from her skills inside the game is going to be epic.

"Fine, princess. Have it your way. But until Chrystal gets here to check you out, *I'm* in charge and there's nothing you can do about it."

We playfully argue until Chrystal arrives and clears her before resetting the game to let the three of us spend a few hours exploring Rora's brand new world.

ACKNOWLEDGMENTS

Fabulous readers, I hope you enjoyed meeting Royce and Rora. I've been dreaming up this story for a long time now and I'm so incredibly excited to have it out in the world!

Special thanks to Elle, Jess, and my incredible team for making this novella happen! I couldn't ask for a better group of people to work with!

Thank you to Yentl and Alexis for tolerating me through cover choices and relentless teasing about what I was writing as I was writing it without actually telling you what I was writing. You ladies rock!

I know this was another surprise book, so thank you to those of you who have stuck with me from the beginning, watching for my little secret releases and jumping on them the moment they come out. You've helped me to accomplish great things in my time as an author and I couldn't be more grateful!

The cool thing is that this originally started out as a short story for an anthology that didn't happen. When I put it out on its own, everyone raved about it so much that I decided to turn it into a novella series. It's all because of your love, emails, and DMs that Rora and Royce's story was given an extended life...we added lives to the game if you want to be technical about it!

The point is that you never know what might happen when you show your favorite author some love!

Keep reading for a first look at more Virtually Sleeping Beauty, as well as find out how to get bonus scenes, play an interactive game for Virtually Sleeping Beauty and more!

Stay inspired,

-K.M. Robinson

BONUS SCENES

WANT TO READ BONUS SCENES FROM K.M. ROBINSON BOOKS? We're giving out exclusive bonus scenes over on the K.M. Robinson Facebook page where you can read scenes from different characters' perspectives from all the stories.

Get them by sending the page a direct message and our bot assistant will get you pointed in the right direction.

We're constantly giving out additional bonus scenes for preorder swag, giveaways, and more, so watch the social media pages carefully for the next scene giveaway.

WORLD PORTALS

READY TO LEARN EXCLUSIVE FACTS ABOUT VIRTUALLY Sleeping Beauty and other K.M. Robinson Series?

World Portals are now available on
www.kmrobinsonbooks.com

Learn behind the scenes facts, watch videos, play games, check out our book filters, find out where to get bonus scenes, view fan art, and get access to other secrets we've hidden away inside the World Portals on the website.

The World Portals are constantly changing and information is being taken away and added all the time, so check back frequently for new content!

LEVEL UP GAME

THINK YOU HAVE WHAT IT TAKES TO SURVIVE AND THRIVE IN Rora's brand new world? Now you can find out!

Join Alan as he takes you through a series of tests to see how you'll handle yourself against knaves, magicians, and dragons before you can enter the virtual reality world with Queen Rora. If you play your cards right, you might find yourself leveling up high enough in the game to earn some bonus lives...or bonus something!

PLAY THE GAME

at

levelupgame.kmrobinsonbooks.com

This game is played directly through Facebook Messenger so you never miss a mission. Alan will send you your tests through your inbox. Have fun running missions to level up inside the virtual reality world to see if you can stand by Queen Rora's side in the castle.

BONUS FACEBOOK FILTERS

WANT TO GET YOUR HANDS ON SOME INCREDIBLE FACEBOOK filters for the K.M. Robinson books? Now you have the ability to get filters for the story, characters, etc right inside your phone.

You can use these on your photos, profile pictures, videos, and live broadcasts. All you have to do is like my author page and they will automatically show up in your filters!

I've even taken these clips and put them on Instagram Stories by saving them to my phone and uploading them to Instagram.

Visit www.facebook.com/kmrobinsonbooks to grab these filters for your photos, videos, and broadcasts! Bonus points for tagging me @kmrobinsonbooks so I can see how you're supporting all of the K.M. Robinson Books.

ABOUT THE AUTHOR

K.M. Robinson is a storyteller who creates new worlds both in her writing and in her fine arts conceptual photography. She is a marketing, branding and social media strategy educator who is recognized at first sight by her very long hair. She is a creative who focuses on photography, videography, couture dress making, and writing to express the stories she needs to tell. She almost always has a camera within reach. Visit her at her website: www. kmrobinsonbooks.com

CONNECT ON SOCIAL MEDIA

facebook.com/kmrobinsonbooks

instagram.com/kmrobinsonbooks

twitter.com/kmrobinsonbooks

Get free excerpts and full novels from K.M. Robinson at
excerpt.kmrobinsonbooks.com

Along Came A Spider: A Prequel Novelette

And They'll Come Home: A Prequel Novelette

The Archives of Jack Frost Series

The Revolution of Jack Frost

The Redemption of Jack Frost (coming soon)

Stealing Steam Series

Book One: Lions and Lamps

Book Two: Pistons and Prisoners

Book Three: Railcars and Rulers

Top Hats and Telegraphs: A Prequel Novella

The Complete Series Boxset/Omnibus with Vambraces and Victories: an exclusive bonus novella

Virtually Sleeping Beauty: A Novella Retelling

The Goose Girl and The Artificial: A Novella Retelling

The Sinking: A Little Mermaid Novella Retelling

Cindrill: A Cinderella Assassin Novella Retelling

Sugarcoated: A Hansel and Gretel's Witch Novella Retelling

JADED: BOOK ONE OF THE JADED DUOLOGY

If the only way to stay alive was to convince your new husband not to murder you and make it look like an accident, could you do it?

At eighteen, Jade shouldn't have to be forced to marry the son of her father's enemy as part of a revenge plot for a failed rebellion. When she's thrown into the life of being the wife of the Commander's son and heir, her only hope for survival is convincing Roan Diamond to actually fall in love with her so that he doesn't kill her on his father's wishes.

While a dutiful son, Roan shouldn't have to trick his new wife into believing his family accepts her, but as the only one in a position to make the country believe Jade is part of their family, he will do what he has to before his family murders his young bride and makes it look like an accident to get back at Jade's father.

With half the country trying to protect Jade and the other half oblivious to the atrocities committed at the Commander's hand, it's a race to see who will win at a deadly game of cat and mouse.

One chooses life. One chooses death. In the midst of chaos, only one will succeed.

Now available!
Learn more about The Jaded Duology at
jadedinfo.kmrobinsonbooks.com

GOLDEN: BOOK ONE OF THE GOLDEN TRILOGY

Goldilocks wasn't naive. She was sent on a mission and Dov Baer is her new target.

When Auluria tricks the Baers into letting her into their home, they have no idea she's actually been sent by the enemy to destroy them. Intent on gathering information for her cousin to hand over to the Society seeking to destroy all of the rebel factions—including her own—she's willing to sacrifice Dov Baer to save her people...until she realizes her cousin lied to her.

Now that she's seen who Dov truly is, she has to decide between staying loyal to her only remaining family or protecting the man she's falling for. If her allegiances are discovered, either side could destroy her—assuming the Society doesn't get her first

Available now!

Learn more about The Golden Trilogy at goldeninfo.
kmrobinsonbooks.com

THE SIREN WARS: BOOK ONE OF THE SIREN WARS SAGA

War has hovered around the kingdom of Scylla for generations ever since the original sirens left the mer collection generations ago after nearly drowning the human prince. Over the years, select mermaids from the royal bloodline have been trained as spies to work for the reigning kings and queens, keeping the collection safe from sirens and humans.

Celena and her partner, Merrick, work covertly for the royals—not even her twin brother knows. When they discover the sirens have broken through the barriers the mer set up to keep the sirens out, Celena and her friends must race to the old kingdom of Metten to stop them from starting a war within their borders.

When she's dragged to the surface, Celena realizes that the

war above the waters is as deadly as the one below the waves—and sacrificing herself may be the only way to protect her family.

The Siren Wars have only just begun.

Available now!
Learn more about The Siren Wars Saga at sirenwarsinfo.kmrobinsonbooks.com

LIONS AND LAMPS: BOOK ONE OF THE STEALING STEAM SERIES

All wishes require sacrifice...*are you willing to pay the price?*

Cyra spent the last seven years being trained to steal an airship in a brutal competition that leaves the victor with millions. Last year, she won.

Aladdin spent the past year fighting to get enough money to take his mother away from Horallen after his father was murdered. Now, his evil uncle Kacper wants to force him into the competition and straight to his death inside the Collection Cave.

When Aladdin discovers a genie said to have been banished a century ago, the competition becomes even deadlier, and he knows he can't trust the girl who snuck into the competition this year...but Cyra might not survive his ruthlessness either in a game where only the lion's heart can win.

All wishes require sacrifice, and someone is going to pay the price for the Stourbridge.

Available now!
Learn more about The Stealing Steam Series at
lionsandlampsinfo.kmrobinsonbooks.com

ALONG CAME A SPIDER: THE FIRST PREQUEL NOVELETTE TO THE LEGENDS CHRONICLES

Little Hacker Muffet

sat on her tuffet

destroying her cords and Way.

Along came a hacker named Spider,

who sat down beside her

and frightened his opponent away.

WHEN FET, ONE OF THE MOST SKILLED HACKERS IN THE Legends, discovers her best friend and leader of her group has been abducted and held for ransom, she must escape unnoticed and find Peep before it's too late.

When Spider, a new recruit training to join her hacker ring, slips out with her and claims to have a plan to save her friend, Fet is forced to bring him along. As she discovers he's not who he claims to be, she faces grave danger and learns just how deadly a spider bite can be.

Now available!
Learn more about The Legends Chronicles at
acasinfo.kmrobinsonbooks.com

VIRTUALLY SLEEPING BEAUTY

To wake her up, he has to enter the game and help her beat it...

Surely the class president wouldn't illegally over-juice to stay in the virtual reality game citizens are allowed to play for four hours a day, but when Royce's aunt calls in a panic because her goddaughter hasn't left the game yet, his only option is to go inside the game and drag the girl out.

The golden knight quickly discovers the princess' absence in the real world isn't of her own doing—*she's trapped inside the game by unknown forces*—and if she can't escape soon, she could die for real outside of the game. He's even more shocked to discover that Rora outranks him inside of the game, which means she'll have to fight to *protect herself* from the evils locking her inside a dangerous world.

Can Rora and Royce work together to outsmart a vicious queen and evil magician, and defeat digital dragons, or will Rora slowly fade away until there's nothing left but an empty shell and the game ranking she will leave behind?

Now available!

Learn more about Virtually Sleeping Beauty at
vsbinfo.kmrobinsonbooks.com

THE REVOLUTION OF JACK FROST

No one inside the snow globe knows that Morozoko Industries is controlling their weather, testing them to form a stronger race that can survive the fall out from the bombs being dropped in the outside world—all they know is that they must survive the harsh Winter that lasts a month and use the few days of Spring, Summer, and Fall to gather enough supplies to survive.

When the seasons start shifting, Genesis and Jack know something is going on. As their team begins to find technology that they don't have access to inside their snow globe of a world, it begins to look more and more like one of their own is working against them.

. . .

Genesis soon discovers Morozoko Industries, but when a foreign enemy tries to destroy their weather program to make sure their destructive life-altering bombs succeed in destroying the outside world, only one person can shut down the machine that is spinning out of control and save the lives of everyone inside the bunker—Jack.

Now available!
Learn more about The Revolution of Jack Frost at
jackfrostinfo.kmrobinsonbooks.com

THE GOOSE GIRL AND THE ARTIFICIAL

WHAT WOULD YOU DO IF YOUR ARTIFICIALLY INTELLIGENT **handmaiden stole your identity?**

Threatened by her Artificial, Arta, Princess Goselyn is forced to switch places and pretend she isn't human when she reaches Prince Corinth to negotiate a treaty they both need to be able to take their respective crowns one day. If she doesn't comply, her Artificial, controlled by her evil cousin, will not only kill Goselyn's mother, but Prince Corinth and his father as well.

Can the quiet princess outsmart a machine created to be more intelligent than she is, all while surviving the other

Artificials and robots working against her in the foreign palace, or will Corinth and his father find out and destroy her chance to save them all?

Learn more about The Goose Girl and The Artificial at
goosegirlinfo.kmrobinsonbooks.com

THE SINKING

The sea witch wants to silence her, but not for the reason you think.

WHEN A QUIRKY OLDER WOMAN PAWNS A FANCY SEASHELL necklace at her mother's antique shop on the pier, Cara doesn't think much about the story the woman spins about the wearer turning into a mermaid.

On her way home, she accidentally drops the necklace into the ocean and is swept out to sea where she meets—a merman who volunteers to take her to his mother, the sea queen, to help her get her legs back.

Cara soon learns that it's Quay's eighteen birthday—a day

that has been a curse for his family—and is meant to be one for her too. Now she must fight to survive the sea with Quay at her side.

Fans of The Little Mermaid will love this twisted take on the beloved story.

Now available!
Learn more about The Sinking at
thesinkinginfo.kmrobinsonbooks.com

CINDRILL

CINDERELLA IS AN ASSASSIN OUT TO MURDER THE PRINCE...*BUT he's hunting her too.*

The nanobots Cindrill's master gives her to use as a mask allow her to slip into the ball wearing a face that isn't hers, but when the assassination attempt goes sideways, Prince Davin doesn't understand why her face changes when he injures her, slicing her foot open around a unique pair of shoes as she runs away.

When Cindrill runs into the prince the next day without her nanobot mask on, he doesn't recognize her, but immediately decides her skills will be useful on his hunt for the would-be-assassin woman who nearly killed his father and his fiancée the night before.

Both are tasked with the job of murdering the other, but things don't quite go as they had planned when Cindrill's master and Davian's fiancée interfere as the two try to decide whether or not to kill the other.

It's hard to recognize a woman when she uses technology to change her appearance, but Cindrill is going to use that to her full advantage as she destroys the prince. *Will either survive?*

Now available!

Learn more about Cindrill at
cindrillinfo.kmrobinsonbooks.com

SUGARCOATED

Hansel and Gretel's witch was actually on their side...

ANNIKA'S JOB IS TO CREATE A CAKE TO MATCH THE CANDY-colored rooftops, nightly firework shows, and daily parades ending in unexpected executions for the mad king's ball, but her true mission is to sneak a thirteen-year-old assassin into the palace using her gift of illusions.

Hansel's job is to protect his little sister, Gretel, once she assassinates King Levin and ends the destruction in Candestrachen, using his power over light to rescue the young girl from the chaos her influence over life and death will create.

When the entire forest reconstructs itself under Gretel's command while trying to save herself from a king's guard,

Hansel and Annika must put their feelings aside and ensure their plan holds true—even if it means one of them has to sacrifice themselves to protect the mission.

Her illusions were meant to save her….but not everyone will survive the assassination attempt.

Learn more about Sugarcoated at
sugarcoatedinfo.kmrobinsonbooks.com

BLOOD IS SILENT

RED RIDING HOOD IS A CIRCUS AERIALIST AND THE WOLF IS ready to cage her.

Sienna has grown up working for the circus, dangling off her signature red silks every night. Her grandmother has been known to wander off to train new acts for their boss, but when Sienna tries to find her to bring her back to the show, she doesn't expect the dashing and dangerous Elijah to join her.

When they finally find Grandma Ida has been transformed deep in the heart of the woods, Sienna will stop at nothing to save her—but the wolf has her right where he wants her, and she won't be able to escape his claws.

. . .

She was told not to go into the woods alone.

Now available!

Learn more about Blood Is Silent at
bloodissilentinfo.kmrobinsonbooks.com